DOG LOVES
BOOKS

LOUISE YATES

Dog loved
books.

He loved
the smell
of them,

and he loved the feel of them.

He loved everything about them.

Dog loved books so much

that he decided to open
his own bookshop.

He unwrapped,

unpacked

and stacked
the books,
ready for the
Grand Opening.

When the day of the
Grand Opening
finally came,
Dog had a bath,

dried his hair,

blew his nose

and threw open the door

to greet his new customers.

But there was no one there.

So Dog tried to keep busy.

And then . . .

a lady came into the shop.

'I'll have a tea with milk and two sugars,'
she said.

"I'm sorry," said Dog, "but this is a bookshop. I only sell books."

The lady walked out.

Dog
was
alone.

He
waited
and
waited.

Then, a man came into the shop . . .

to ask for directions.

When he left, Dog was downhearted.

But not for long!

He wouldn't wait a
moment more.

Dog fetched a book from the shelf
and began to read.

When he read,
he forgot
that he was
waiting.

When he read,
he forgot that
he was alone.

When he read,
he forgot that
he was in the
bookshop.

And when one adventure ended, Dog simply took another book down from the shelf and . . .

a new
adventure began!

So Dog was somewhere else
altogether when . . .

a customer came into the shop to ask
for a book.

Dog knew
exactly
which
ones to
recommend.

but most of all . . .

he loves to share them!

For Eleanor and Cedric

DOG LOVES BOOKS
A RED FOX BOOK 978 1 862 30695 0

Published in hardback by Jonathan Cape. Simultaneously published in paperback by Red Fox,
an imprint of Random House Children's Publishers UK
A Random House Group Company

This edition published 2010

7 9 10 8 6

Red Fox Books are published by Random House Children's Publishers UK,
61–63 Uxbridge Road, London W5 5SA

www.randomhousechildrens.co.uk

Addresses for companies within The Random House Group Limited can be found at: www.randomhouse.co.uk/offices.htm

THE RANDOM HOUSE GROUP Limited Reg. No. 954009

A CIP catalogue record for this book is available from the British Library.

Printed in Malaysia